JP
MOSS

Moss, Miriam.
Bad hare day.

For everyone who's had a bad hair day – and Janine *MM*

For Joshua *LC*

MY 21 '03   Text copyright © 2003 by Miriam Moss
Illustrations copyright © 2003 by Lynne Chapman

Published by Bloomsbury, New York and London
Distributed to the trade by Holtzbrinck Publishers

Library of Congress Cataloging-in-Publication Data:
Moss, Miriam
Bad hare day / by Miriam Moss; illustrated by Lynne Chapman. p.cm.
Summary: Uncle Herbert the Hare, the best hairdresser in town, has his hands full
when his niece Holly spends time at his salon.
ISBN 1-58234-785-9 (alk. paper)
[1. Hairdressing—Fiction. 2. Behavior—Fiction. 3. Uncles—Fiction. 4. Hares—Fiction.
5. Animals—Fiction.] I. Chapman, Lynne, 1960- ill. II. Title.
PZ7.M85353 Bad 2003
[E]—dc21
2002026228

First U.S. Edition 2003
Printed in Hong Kong

1 3 5 7 9 10 8 6 4 2

Bloomsbury USA Children's Books
175 Fifth Avenue
New York, New York 10010

bad hare day

by Miriam Moss
illustrated by Lynne Chapman

BLOOMSBURY
CHILDREN'S
BOOKS

Herbert Hare was a hairdresser. The best in town.

Everyone came from miles around to be styled, sculpted, cut or conditioned by Herbert.

Inside his salon all was calm.
Soft music played, fans whirred
and the coffee machine hummed.

Clink! A chair was raised.
Snip! Soft hair slithered to the ground.
Swish! The assistant swept it up.

"Now who's coming today?" asked Herbert looking in his book one March morning.

"A wash and blow dry for Bear,

a feathered cut
for Colobus,

a perm for Panda

and long layers for Llama."

"And that's just the beginning!" said Herbert, throwing open
the doors with a flourish.

On the sidewalk outside stood Holly, Herbert's niece.
"Hello," she said. "Mama says you should look after
me while she goes shopping."
"Oh!" said Herbert. "I hope you'll be good."

Holly climbed onto a seat
and opened a magazine.
"I'm sure I shall," she said.

While Herbert was busy brushing Bear's hair,
Holly helped herself to a drink.
First a cup of hot chocolate, then a raspberry
milk, then a herb tea, then a mixture of all three.

Chocolate

Herb Tea

Raspberry Milk

Coffee

Holly kept playing with the buttons – until
the machine was completely empty.

"Shampoo delivery." shouted a man
in overalls from the back door.

Herbert and his
assistant scurried off to
sort out the stock room.

While Herbert was away, Holly cleaned the mirrors
with fine sprays and chatted to the customers.
Then she adjusted the controls on the hood dryer.

The line grew.

Helpful Holly sat everyone down in a row.
Then she went up and down,
shaving a neck here,

snipping a beard there

and fixing Bald
Eagle's new wig.

Holly bleached out
Badger's stripes

and gave
Orangutan
a terribly
tight perm.

"Who's next?" she called, waving over Cockatoo, Cormorant and Crane.

Llama wanted
long layers,
but she got
short bangs.

Colobus wanted
a feathered cut
but he got stubble.

Holly the hairdresser was in full swing. She herded Lion, Flamingo, Moose and Bear from the hair washing area to be blow dried. She volumised Lion's mane, fluffed Flamingo up to three times her size, moussed Moose and backcombed Bear.

"There! All finished!" she said, clapping
her hands delightedly, just as …

... Herbert hopped up the steps
from the back of the salon.
"What HAVE you done!"
cried Herbert, "You
bad, bad hare."

Holly looked up at her uncle
with sad, big brown eyes.
"I was only trying to help,"
she said, slipping
her paw into his.

At that moment the salon doors swung open.
"Darlings! Have you had a lovely time?"

Mama dropped
her shopping.

"Good heavens, Herbert!" she cried.
"What happened?"
Herbert looked down at Holly.
"Let's just say it's been a
bad hare day," he said.